PRESIDENT MICHELLE

OR

TEN DAYS THAT SHOOK THE WORLD

PRESIDENT MICHELLE

OR

TEN DAYS THAT SHOOK THE WORLD

A SUBVERSIVE POLITICAL FANTASY

MANU HERBSTEIN

This book is a work of fiction.

ISBN 978-9988-2-3307-5

Also by Manu Herbstein

Ama, a Story of the Atlantic Slave Trade
Brave Music of a Distant Drum
The Boy who Spat in Sargrenti's Eye
Akosua and Osman
Ramseyer's Ghost

PREFACE

A long time ago I took an oath never to write anything inoffensive...the single characteristic that most makes a difference in the success of an article...is the author's courage in revealing normally unspoken things about... his society. It takes guts to be a writer...What makes writing at its best interesting is the writer's willingness to broach the unspeakable...the best writers, those whose originality shines, tend to be those who are most outspoken.
Sol Stein, *Stein on Writing, Guts: The Decisive Ingredient*

This story is wholly fictional. Barack Obama did not die of a heart attack in the run-up to the 2012 Presidential election. Joe Biden did not succeed him. The Democratic Convention was not recalled. Jesse Jackson did not propose and Hillary Clinton did not nominate Michelle Obama as the party's new candidate.

The whole story of Michelle Obama's election as President of the United States in 2012 is a figment of my imagination. I have no reason to believe that Mrs. Obama espouses the political agenda that I have attributed to her.

The passing references to other celebrities, including Rush Limbaugh and Sarah Palin, are also inventions.

If apologies are due to any of the real persons who feature in this story, I make them now.

I wrote this story in the closing months of 2009. A friend wrote from Washington D.C., "On your fantasy, I can't imagine that any major magazine editor would publish—at least I hope not."

He was right: I failed to identify any publisher who shared my view that this story would be of interest to American readers. I self-published it for the Kindle on May 30, 2011, setting the price at $0.99. The only time it was downloaded was on the days when it was free. It has had just one review, of which more below

My Washington correspondent, a strong supporter of Barack Obama wrote, "…There's just no chance the political agenda you attribute to Michelle could be realized and no evidence that it would be her agenda. Kucinich is not popular. You can't get any legislation through the Senate in 10 days unless it's enormously popular, if then. Your political agenda just is not the US's, no matter what its merits may be. And some aspects of it might well be ruled unconstitutional. So yes, it is a subversive fantasy! And it is shared by some here, but not many."

Seven years later, Bernie Sanders' success in the Democratic Party primary campaign suggests that elements of the fictional agenda I attribute to Michelle Obama do indeed have quite substantial grass-roots support, especially amongst young voters.

My single reviewer wrote, "Sections of [the story] had me well up in tears as I pondered how far we are from the ideals the book contemplates. This e-book captures the energy and expectations of a class of people around the world who once suspected that President Obama might himself have been the harbinger of a radically revolutionary type of leadership. In their disappointment, this fictionalized President Michelle Obama may help preserve some sense of hope in a politically bleak (and certainly non-revolutionary) performance by the historic president Obama."

If Bernie Sanders, at 79, proves to be too old to mount a renewed challenge to Hillary Clinton in 2020, another champion of that agenda will surely emerge. Might that champion be the real-life Michelle Obama rather than the fictional Michelle Obama of this story?

Manu Herbstein, Accra, Ghana, October 14, 2016.

ONE

The President said she had been asked how she would prefer to be addressed. She suggested that "President Obama" be reserved for her late husband. "President Michelle Obama" struck her as too formal.

"If you can't bring yourself to call the President of the United States of America plain "Michelle," she said, "I suggest that you call me 'President Michelle.'"

The 2012 campaign was well under way when Barack Obama succumbed to a sudden heart attack. Vice-President Biden was sworn in as President and the Democratic Party recalled its convention to confirm him as its presidential candidate in the forthcoming election. Jumping the gun, Sarah Palin, the Republican candidate, lost no time in launching an unseemly, ill-considered and, as it turned out, futile attack on Biden.

Her attack was futile because the opinion polls gave the Democrats pause for thought. Whereas the first national debate had earned President Obama a fifteen-point lead over Palin, the polls suggested that a Biden-Palin trial of strength might be a close call. Jesse Jackson made a powerful speech proposing that the Democratic Party select Michelle Obama as its candidate to succeed her late husband. In the event, there was no contest: Hillary Clinton made the nomination, as she had done for Barack

Obama in 2008, and Michelle was selected by acclamation. She made a short, dignified, acceptance statement—one could hardly call it a speech—over a video link. She said she accepted the nomination with humility as a duty to the nation. She apologized for her failure to attend the convention in person. She was sure that the delegates would respect her need for private time to mourn her husband. She nominated Joe Biden as her running mate.

Michelle took no public part in the 2012 campaign. Leaving everything to the nationwide network of supporters who had come to know her well enough during her husband's brilliant 2008 campaign, she made no speeches, no appearances. She declined to take part in the two remaining scheduled debates. Sarah Palin was left to tilt at a non-existent windmill. She accused Michelle of irresponsibility, of asking the voters to give her a blank check; and much else. And that was the end of her. The sentimental American electorate was disarmed by images of the black-clad Michelle and her two orphaned daughters. Rush Limbaugh's diatribes outraged all but a fanatical fringe. The mainstream media found it difficult to do other than echo the sentiments revealed by the polls.

It was not that the American people trusted Michelle or, indeed, mistrusted her. Rather, in a manner that only a few dissident commentators at the time perceived and described as sexist, they saw her as a political carbon copy of her husband, a female Barack Obama. Time would tell how wrong they were.

How wrong they were, indeed. For President Michelle has proved herself a totally different politician. Whereas Barack Obama was a middle of the road reconciler, a would-be president-for-all-the-people, trying desperately to create a consensus for his program of mild reforms, Michelle's performance to date reveals her as an ideologue, a pragmatic ideologue it is true, but demonstrably committed to policies based on principles. She chooses to describe those principles as simple Christian moral values. Her critics prefer to label them with that worst of American insults: socialist.

Michelle's campaign was run by much the same multi-talented team that had propelled her husband to the White House. Four years older now, but more than four years wiser, they were determined that this time the "change" promised by Barack in 2008 would prove to be much more than just a slogan. The word from the White House, where Michelle was still living, was encouraging.

Almost the first thing the campaigners did was to establish an independent communications network, a private Internet. It has been a key to their success and, in spite of much rumor and speculation, impervious to penetration.

By a consensual process that remains obscure, they established several brain trusts and ensconced them in remote retreats. The membership of the brain trusts, as far as we know, comprised the cream of the American left, some registered Democrats, some not, ranging in age from the low twenties to the high eighties, but mostly young. The Network evidently permitted them to communicate with one another and with the candidate in conditions of secrecy.

Conspiracy theorists have speculated that Michelle issued no instruction of any import without running it past the incisive intellect of an old friend and trusted mentor who had moved into the White House unobserved. Journalists seeking him out at his home to solicit his comments on Michelle's candidacy were told that he had travelled abroad and was not expected to return until after the election.

The first brain trust framed a program of action for the new administration, constructing a foundation upon which the other committees worked.

It drew up lists of candidates for cabinet posts and other presidential appointments and drafted documents outlining domestic and foreign policy and a consistent approach to issues of war and peace; and economic and environmental policy; and so on. In each group, a sub-committee began to outline legislation. The outcomes of this work are slowly emerging but for the full story we may have await publication of the participants' memoirs.

At this time, then, the history of the campaign cannot be other than of a provisional nature.

The results of the election are on record: Michelle Obama won a landslide victory and the Democratic Party achieved substantial majorities in both houses of Congress.

The plotters must surely have rejoiced, but in private. To disclose their program at this stage, they must have reasoned, would have been to court disaster. So there was no phased hand-over from the previous administration, no transition. Their performance demonstrates a determination to start with a clean slate, to deny the old guard any influence. In the meantime, they allowed President Biden to stumble along until the date of President Michelle's inauguration.

TWO

A personal note. Shortly before the Inauguration, I had delivered the final corrected draft of my latest book to my publisher. I had promised my wife, Clara, that once this was done we would head off for a quiet few days together in the cabin we own up in the mountains. I tried to negotiate a postponement ("Don't you want to watch the Inauguration?") but Clara wasn't having any. So we delivered the kids to my parents, set the answer-phone and the video, switched off our cell-phones, and off we went. (Yes, thanks, we had a glorious couple of days together.) We got back late at night on the day after the Inauguration, too late to call the kids. Dog-tired, we took a shower and turned in.

I was up early the next morning. I ran the DVD of the Inauguration and Michelle's Day 2 address to Congress with the sound turned down while I called the kids and made breakfast.

I teach political science and draw most of my lecture material from current news. Later, I would watch again, marking up the transcript and making notes.

Clara came down, grabbed a cup of coffee, called the kids and rushed off to work. Then I made myself comfortable and watched Michelle's speech again. Wow! What a challenge for my students. As I'd worked on building up my lecture notes for the next semester, I'd guessed there was something unusual afoot, but this was beyond my wildest expectations. Four years ago, practically every leading economist got it all wrong. This time around it seems that it's the turn of the political scientists. So much for the wisdom of academics.

It must have been near noon when I got around to checking the messages on the answer phone. Most of them were from Ted, my agent. "Bob, where the hell are you? Have you switched off your cell-phone? Call me back at once." The calls were repeated at 30-minute intervals and the level of hysteria increased with each. That hysteria echoed, he was to tell me, the mood of New York publishers. Anything with a sexy picture of the President on the cover and a title like *The First Hundred Days* was going to be their salvation in a shrinking market. They were scraping the academic barrel. Even post-doctorals were being offered unheard-of advances. The tone of Ted's last message was plaintive. "Bob, where are you? Please call me. I implore you." Then they stopped. He must have been badly in need of sleep.

I called him. When he calmed down, he told me the deal. The title was to be President Michelle: the First Ten Days. We were already half way through Day 3. I was to e-mail my manuscript not later than midnight on Day 12, February 1. The print machines would start running the following morning. The publisher had already lined up reviewers, who would work on the digital files without waiting for the galleys. By Day 15 the books would be on display at the entrance of every Barnes and Noble and Walmart Branch. All they needed was an author. Me.

I should have said no, but a generous six figure advance is not something a struggling academic can afford to sniff at; and I already had my campaign notes to build on. I phoned Clara and asked her to lay in stocks of coffee. No disturbances. The kids would move to their maternal grandparents.

I called my Dean. And then I got to work. If this strikes you as a potboiler, full of much speculation and long passages lifted straight from the transcript, I hope you'll understand.

THREE

In the short victory speech in which she thanked the American people for electing her, President-elect Michelle Obama undertook to disclose her policies and appointments immediately after her inauguration. Until then, she asked for patience. In view of the dire state of the economy and the fact that she was still in mourning, she decreed that there would be no celebratory balls and that the inauguration ceremony would be simple.

Starved of facts, the media filled pages and airtime with speculation.

True, there were no formal balls, but two million Americans, young and old, partied in the Mall throughout the eve of the Inauguration. The prohibition on tents had been relaxed.

Packed coaches rolled in day and night, festooned with flags and home town banners. Celebrated musicians performed free of charge and ambitious youngsters rapped or strummed or read their verses on improvised platforms.

Great video screens displayed the swearing-in. Bringing her brief remarks to a close, President Michelle asked those who could to stay on.

"I might need your help," she said, as if in jest. "Be prepared to stay for at least a week."

The campaign network was made flesh. Activists tramped the grounds, hugging and slapping, exploring minds and arguing tactics and strategy and policy. Many felt that they had been let down the last time around. They were determined to do all it took to prevent a repeat.

At eight on Day 2, President Michelle arrived to address a combined session of the House of Representatives and the Senate. Nationwide, work stopped. In factories and offices, in transport cafes and in the homes of the unemployed (those who still had homes) Americans watched and listened.

Dressed in mourning, as she had been since the death of her husband, Michelle stepped across to the podium. Her feet hidden from the cameras, she slipped out of her high heels and into more comfortable footwear.

Smiling, she spoke first of her devotion to her late husband.

"Great American that he was," she said, "he did his utmost to lead this nation along a broad highway of reform."

"Better than anyone," she continued, "I know how committed he was to building a national consensus and how sad he was that the Right refused to reciprocate the concessions he made to them."

"I do not propose to travel that same road," she said. "The people of the United States have given me and my party a mandate. I intend to exercise that mandate by pursuing a radical program."

Radical? That could mean anything. The legislators applauded politely. Only a trusted few had any inkling of what she had in store for them. But she made them wait, devoting the next hour to the delivery of a history lesson.

She paid tribute first to the Native Peoples of the Americas, "the original owners of these lands." The continents they inhabited had been stolen from them by successive waves of European settlers. Their determined resistance had been overcome by the superior firepower and insatiable greed of the invaders. (At this, some legislators were seen to shift on their buttocks.)

Then she moved on to the four-hundred-year history of the

trans-Atlantic slave trade. Again, the perpetrators were almost all Europeans. In this case the victims were all Africans. Some of them were her own ancestors.

Again she paid tribute, this time to those who had resisted enslavement, and to the successive generations who had confronted the denial of their human dignity and rights; and she paid tribute too to those who had fought for the abolition of slavery.

"Throughout the Americas," she said, "and in Africa too, the psychological, social and economic scars of this history stubbornly persist."

The TV cameras picked up some heads nodding in agreement and some clearly at odds with her interpretation of American history.

"The economy of the United States," she said, "was founded upon the expropriation of land and labor, land from those whom we now call Native Americans and labor from unwilling immigrants from Africa."

At this stage one legislator, later identified as a Republican Senator, stood up, bowed to the Chair, and left the chamber. The TV cameras picked up heads turning to watch his exit. Was this some sort of protest, or just nature's urgent call? It wasn't clear.

The President undertook to establish a committee of experts to advise her on whether it would be appropriate to compensate the descendants of the victims of what would today be regarded as crimes against humanity; and what form such compensation might take. Her own preference was for a Truth and Reconciliation Commission on the South African model, but she would not attempt to influence the committee's conclusions and recommendations. She said she would charge the same committee with advising her as to how future U.S. domestic and foreign policy might take account of this past history.

"One of the most pernicious, humiliating and degrading aspects of slavery," she continued, "still persists in the United States. I shall initiate legislation outlawing the use of iron chains and shackles for the restraint of human beings in any circumstances. I propose that a nation-wide collection of such chains be made and that they be piled up in the open, perhaps near the Lincoln Memorial and left there to rust."

Another Republican bowed and left the chamber; and then another. The President watched them, waiting until they were out of sight before proceeding.

"For too long," she said, "we have lacked the courage to confront our past. We need to learn to talk to one another about our history. In so doing, we may learn to shed the unacknowledged burdens of guilt and shame and pain which inform our daily lives."

Many of the minority Republicans and some of the Democrats too were clearly uncomfortable with all this. This was not the American history they had learned at school and college. What the President said next suggests that she must have sensed this discomfort. She put her papers to one side.

"I don't want you to misunderstand me," she said. "I am not accusing anyone now living of the crimes of our forebears. And I say 'our.' This is not a black-white issue. In spite of the continuing inequalities in our society, we all benefit in some way from the crimes and suffering of our respective ancestors. My purpose in raising these issues in this forum is to establish a firm basis for everything I and my administration plan to do during my term of office, a basis of honesty and respect for human dignity and human rights. And not only in America. In all the world."

She held up a hand to stop the applause.

"What I am tentatively staking out here today," she said, "is a case for leadership, for American leadership. But leadership of a different kind, leadership based not on economic and military power. No. Not that. Not that. I ask, with all humility, that my leadership be judged and that this country's leadership be judged, from this day on, on moral grounds."

The ovation started slowly, with the progressives. They rose to their feet. Their fellow Democrats followed. Embarrassed, the Republicans, aware of television cameras, could not but do likewise. Only a few stalwarts remained glued to their seats.

10

Out on the Mall, the activists turned from the giant video screens and exchanged ecstatic high-fives.

President Michelle took a sip of water. Then she turned and beckoned. An aide brought her a high stool.

"I'm not used to delivering long orations," she said. "I hope I'm not boring you. Now where was I?"

She had not quite finished her lecture. She now recited a long list of the United States' major military interventions in foreign lands, starting with Haiti, Hawaii, the Philippines, Puerto Rico and Cuba in the nineteenth century and working up to Iran, Korea, Vietnam, Libya, Sudan and Somalia, in more recent times.

Turning to Iraq, she said that few would dispute that Saddam Hussein was a nasty piece of work.

"But was that sufficient justification for invading his country?" she asked. "Our government evidently thought not, for they found it necessary to deceive us with a crudely concocted fiction about weapons of mass destruction."

Saddam Hussein's Iraq had been no Garden of Eden but, for all his many faults, he had held his country together.

"Today," she said, "millions of Iraqis are still in exile, afraid to go home. Individually and collectively, they are a nation traumatized by conflict."

She invited a moment's reflection of what their condition might be today had we never invaded their country. Iraqis might well still be living under a dictatorship, she surmised. Tough. But many now dead or in exile would still be alive, living in their own homes, facing the challenge of initiating and conducting their own struggle for freedom and democracy.

"We must accept our share of the responsibility, which is the major share, for the tragic condition of Iraq and its people today," she said.

She promised to set up another independent judicial committee, this time to investigate the origins of the decision to invade Iraq and its consequences.

Three more legislators left the chamber. She watched them go.

Then, evidently departing from her prepared speech, she announced that the United States would shortly submit itself to the jurisdiction of the International Criminal Court.

"While on that issue," she said, "I shall take whatever steps are necessary to deal with the long overdue ratification of other international treaties such as the U.N. Convention on the Rights of the Child."

Afghanistan and Pakistan were next. There again, we had lost our way. Our declared intention had been to apprehend our erstwhile protégé, Osama bin Laden. The President was not persuaded that, with sufficient diplomatic and economic pressure, the Taliban government might not have handed him over or at least expelled him from his sanctuary in their country. They might well have condoned his behavior, but she knew of no evidence that the Taliban were a direct party to the plot that led to 9/11.

"Much of the culture of the Taliban is anathema to me, particularly its attitude to the rights of women. But was it our task to set them right? Did President George W. Bush and Vice-President Dick Cheney and their cohort of neo-cons tell us that what we were undertaking was regime change in the interests of social reform in a distant land?" she asked.

"The principal of Manifest Destiny," she said, "seems to run like a thread through American history. For my part, deeply committed Christian that I am, I do not believe that God has charged the United States of America with the task of being the world's policeman."

Turning to the domestic economy, President Michelle addressed the enormous disparity in wealth and income between the small class of extremely rich Americans and the large underclass of the unemployed and poorly paid. She said she had been called a socialist, but that was not true. She had no doubt, she said, that, at a certain level, the market was the best, the most efficient mechanism, for regulating the economy.

"But," she said, "let me share a secret with you. Like the Republican right, I dislike big government. Big government, however, is reasonably transparent. It is under constant observation by those whom the American people regularly send to this building to represent them; and by the media. Big business however, big oil, big armaments, big coal, big banking, big business is another matter entirely. Big business is largely lacking in transparency. And yet, as the 2008 melt-down of our economy demonstrated, policy decisions made behind the closed doors of boardrooms, supposedly in the interest of shareholders, but often in the interest of the managers responsible to no one but themselves, can have disastrous effects on the lives and well-being of the rest of us."

She said she was all in favor of bonuses. She planned to propose a new scheme of national awards that would recognize and reward citizens who made distinguished contributions to the well-being of the American people and humankind, in all fields, teaching, nursing, the arts, inventions, to name just a few. But huge bonuses, granted as rewards for making profits through speculation, would be the subject of a new tax regime. Bonuses granted in recognition of good productive work, not gambling skill, and which were a reasonable proportion of salary, would not be affected.

One of her highest priorities, President Michelle said, would be to see to it that every American who was willing and able to work, had a job. The market economy had failed to achieve this, which was not surprising since its primary objective was to make profits, not to satisfy social needs.

"I regard unemployment as an avoidable social ill, not as an impersonal market factor," she said.

Some of the nation's elected representatives continued to shift in their seats. Two more departed from the chamber. Out on the Mall, everything the new President said raised a mighty cheer.

She passed now to a review of distortions in American society that resulted from what she characterized as "the prevailing ideology of laissez faire."

"We treasure our individual freedoms," she said. "Yet we are unable to fashion means to control assaults on those freedoms by purveyors of pornography, substance abuse, gun crime, identity theft and spam. And then we display a total lack of imagination by using incarceration in prison as the only means of punishing non-violent crime. Our approach to violent crime is equally ineffective. More than 1 in 100 of our citizens, well over 2 million Americans, are in prison. We have 5% of the world's population but nearly a quarter of the world's prison population. The United States leads the world when it comes to incarceration. Of the major nations, China comes second, but it is a long, long way behind. That is a national disgrace that, I promise you, will not survive my term of office. I'm not yet sure how to deal with it, but we will find a way."

"I hate to say this," she said, "but honesty demands it. American society is broke. Broke. In both senses of that word."

She ran her gaze over the assembled legislators.

"With your support and with the support of the American people," she said, "I intend to fix it."

She arranged her papers and took a drink of water while she waited for the applause to subside. Watching her, some of the Democratic Party legislators might have reflected that this seemed to be a very different Michelle Obama than the woman and wife who had addressed them at the 2008 convention. They had given her a blank check and she seemed intent on cashing it.

"I think that's enough for one day," she said. "My girls are due home from school shortly and I need to get their lunch."

FOUR

Vice-president Joe Biden was shown in. The girls were sitting at one end of the dining table doing their homework. He leaned down to give each of them a kiss. The seat at the head of the table was empty. Michelle sat to the right of the empty chair, still dressed as she had been at the Capitol that morning. Opposite her, wearing a pullover, sat the Rev. Jeremiah Wright. Biden hid his astonishment. Wright rose to greet him. Michelle offered to introduce them but it wasn't necessary: they had met before.

I can't vouch for the truth of this story. All I can say is I heard it on Capitol Hill and it seems authentic.

FIVE

That evening several of the protesting Republican legislators (for such they proved to be) were interviewed on television and radio. They all expressed, some in strong language, their deep concern about the direction in which they alleged President Michelle was leading the country. One went so far as to suggest that we were in the midst of a real life rerun of the movie *The Manchurian Candidate*.

"Are you suggesting that the President has been brain-washed?" asked the astonished interviewer.

The Senator nodded.

"By whom? The Chinese? Al-Qaeda?"

The Senator refused to speculate.

Later that night the Republican legislators met, so we have learned, with Sarah Palin in the chair. Her position in the party had been undermined by her poor performance in the campaign and her failure in the election. Some chat show hosts were suggesting that the President's speech that morning could only strengthen her position. There have been no leaks from that meeting but the outcome became clear in the course of the following day.

SIX

Next morning, I caught the Acela Express from Penn Station and settled down to watch the show in the Capitol on the screen of my laptop.

The anchors introduced the occasion over a backdrop of images of early risers on the Mall rubbing their hands before their charcoal braziers and brewing tea and coffee. Shortly before eight, the large video screens lit up, showing the scene inside the Capitol.

The late-comers were still taking their seats when the President arrived. She wore a white, sleeveless dress, stylish in its simplicity. Responding to the symbolism, the Democrats rose to their feet and gave her a standing ovation. The Republicans had little choice but to follow suit. She smiled and nodded her head in acknowledgment.

Outside, the crowd rose too and at once began to chant the campaign slogan "President Michelle, President Michelle."

"Madam Speaker," she said, raising her hands for silence.

The legislators took their seats.

"Madam Speaker," she repeated. "I have an important announcement to make."

The previous evening, she told them, Vice-President Joe Biden had called on her and submitted a formal letter of resignation.

The TV cameras picked up the astonishment on the faces of the legislators.

They had agreed, she told them, that for the time being the contents of President Biden's letter would remain confidential. She was free to say, however, that it contained assurances of his continuing support. Their warm personal relationship would in no way be impaired and she expected to continue to benefit from his advice.

She paid tribute to the service which Joe Biden had rendered to the nation, as Senator, as Vice-President to her late husband and as President.

"In the course of the next few days," she announced, "I shall be seeking advice from a broad spectrum of opinion as to whom I should nominate to fill the office of the 49th Vice President of the United States."

Picked up by the cameras, the faces of many legislators, both Democrats and Republicans, appeared disturbed. My guess is that they saw Joe Biden as a guarantee of some continuity and stability in a time of radical change, a steadying hand on the wheel of a vehicle driven by a learner driver.

Out on the Mall, the activist campaigners made no secret of their delight.

The cameras picked up frenetic activity in the crowded press gallery.

All over the country rich men made desperate efforts to reach their stockbrokers. The Dow Jones and the Nasdaq appeared to be in free fall.

President Michelle waited patiently for the buzz to subside. Then she continued, "I have responsibilities other than the Presidency. I am a mother, now, sadly, a single mother. I intend to continue to devote quality time to my daughters every day. I will discuss their homework with them and attend meetings of the PTA at their school. I propose to be a somewhat hands-off president. The hands on will those of my Vice. The person I choose will have to fit that bill."

"Now to business," she said. "On your desks each of you will find a sealed brown paper parcel, addressed to you but marked 'Not to be opened without the permission of the President.' I hope none of you has jumped the gun. Have you? Anyone? Hands up anyone who has opened his parcel!"

Abashed, an elderly Senator raised his hand. His fellows looked at one another and smiled indulgently.

The President wagged a school-marmish finger at the culprit. Senator X bowed his head.

"When I say go," she said, "you may open the parcels, but not before. When you do so you will find inside four books and two bound volumes.

"The books, suitably inscribed, are a modest personal gift from me to each of you to mark my assumption of office. Let me emphasize that this gift is not a bribe! I expect no favors in return. After considerable thought I selected *Bury My Heart at Wounded Knee* by the late Dee Brown, Howard Zinn's *A People's History of the United States*, Barack Obama's *Dreams of My Father* and Lewis Carrol's *Alice in Wonderland*, a favorite since my childhood and a book which I have read and re-read with my daughters. If you've read some or all of them, I beg you to do so again, but whether you do so or not I ask you to treat this gift as a mark of my friendship and esteem. I'm a bibliophile. I would have loved to have given each of you a whole library. But then I guess that most of you share my love of books and already have large libraries of your own.

"In the first bound volume will find a list of 350 of our fellow citizens whom I propose, subject to the approval of the Senate, to appoint to cabinet posts and other positions of major responsibility. You will find for each nominee a statement from me justifying my nomination, a detailed curriculum vitae and a policy statement from the nominee, setting out the priorities which we have together established."

She said that she had broken with tradition in delaying this submission until after her inauguration. Given the many important tasks that awaited the urgent attention of her administration, she urged the Senators to consider her nominations and approve them with the minimum possible delay.

"My guess," she said, "is that you will find the names of many, if not most, of my nominees unfamiliar. When they appear before you, you may also be struck by the fact that few of them are older than forty and many of them are much younger."

In spite of their youth, she said, each one of them would be able to demonstrate at his or her selection hearings in the Senate all the necessary qualities for the post. She said she was satisfied that every one of them was a person of high integrity and commitment.

"For every generation of politicians," she said, "there comes a time when they must hand over the reins of government to younger folk, people with fresh ideas, relevant to the contemporary world. This is such a time."

"Madam Speaker," she continued, "I have only one political debt to pay and that is to the American people who have elected me. As you know, I took no public part in the campaign. I made it known that I needed a period of withdrawal and peace with my daughters to mourn my husband and their father. While that was wholly true, one unintended and unforeseen consequence is that I have, apart from that one debt, no others, certainly no monetary debts, but also no political debts, not to individuals, not to any corporation or lobby or any other special interest group. I am my own man, my own woman."

The second bound volume, she told them, contained drafts of a number of laws that she asked them to study and debate at the earliest possible opportunity. Of these, she said, she attached the highest priority to the first. There would be time to address the others once Congress had sent this one to her for signature.

SEVEN

President Michelle's first draft bill had the provocative title *An Act to Restore Democracy to the United States of America.*

"Some of you," she told the legislators, "have been able to fund your election campaigns from your own private fortunes. The campaigns of others have been funded through donations, some from private individuals, some from corporations and others from the special interest groups we know as lobbies.

"Some corporations hedge their bets by donating large sums to both major parties. Let us not deceive ourselves: they do not make these donations from a selfless love of democracy; they do so in order to advance their own interests, interests which, given the nature of our system, are more narrowly focused."

She challenged every elected representative to search his or her conscience. They had been elected to serve the interests of the people of the United States of America.

"Is your obligation to your electors," she asked them, "the sole obligation which determines your voting record?"

"Please don't misunderstand me," she said, scanning the faces before her.

"I am not accusing any of you of misconduct. The fault, as I see it, is systemic. The system which has grown up by stealth since the Second World War, bears little resemblance to that envisaged by the writers of our Constitution. The years since the administration of President Eisenhower have seen an inexorable growth in the corrosive, corrupting influence of what he called the military-industrial complex."

The *Act to Restore Democracy*, she claimed, would not only halt that trend but also reverse it. The Act would make it an offence for any candidate for public office to accept gifts or loans in support of his or her election campaign; or, indeed, to use personal wealth for such a purpose. Congress would allocate funds to an Independent Electoral Authority and this Authority would in turn fund the electoral campaigns of all candidates qualified to stand for office.

The Act would set up a National Broadcasting Corporation, publicly owned and financed, but independently managed. All candidates for election would be entitled to a free allocation of television and radio time. Checks against abuse would be built in to the system.

At a stroke, this law would level the electoral playing field. For the first time in generations the wealthy would have little or no advantage over the poor in the competition for office. She expected new talents to emerge which would enrich and invigorate American political life. New parties might enter the political arena, breaking the monopoly presently shared by Republicans and Democrats and breathing new life into American democracy.

"Distinguished members of the Senate and the House," she said, "these new rules might cause discomfort to some of you. If so, I apologize for the discomfort, though not for the rules and the principle they embody."

She paused to allow them time for reflection. Then she suggested that before they made up their minds, they should all take a walk outside and listen to the views of their fellow citizens who had been camping on the Mall, braving the winter weather because of their commitment to seeing this Bill become law.

They must surely have guessed what she was doing. The deep vested interest that most members of Congress and the

Senate, of both parties, had in the status quo was well known, not least to the legislators themselves. President Michelle had recently been elected to office with an overwhelming and unprecedented majority. She was now making a bold, indeed outrageous, threat to appeal directly to her voters, represented by the crowds on the Mall, over the heads of their elected legislators. In a sense, this was a magnificent bluff. American voters are essentially conservative in their outlook. They had voted for the person of President Michelle, not for the radical program which she was now launching. Her strength was the high moral ground she was making her own; and the crowds outside. But these were almost certainly an untypical sample of the electorate. An intensely interesting battle for the soul of the American people was under way.

The President invited the legislators to give the draft their urgent critical attention. Speaking directly to the cameras, she invited the same attention from the millions of voters camped on the lawns outside the Capitol, gathered in town-hall meetings throughout the country and watching on television in their homes and work places. Many of the legislators must have shuddered at the implied threat of being bypassed by the President's direct appeal to a popular power base remote from the traditional seat of legislative power in Washington.

"Before I leave you to your deliberations," the President continued, "Let me return, briefly, to the short policy statements in your nominees file. You will find there, proposals for some major changes. Each of these merits, indeed demands, extended debate, both inside the House of Representatives and the Senate and nationwide. Right now, I shall do no more than list the most notable.

"Before I do so, however, let me make a firm commitment. I have no intention of standing for a second term. While I shall watch the opinion polls, the stock markets and the economic statistics with interest, I shall not allow myself to be unduly swayed by such short term influences. While I shall pay close attention to all sober and constructive advice and criticism, my firm intention is to lead not to follow.

"Now to policy. Foreign policy first.

"I shall bring all our troops home from both Iraq and Afghanistan as soon as practicable. That last phrase, let me emphasize, is not an escape clause. If I could bring them home tomorrow, I would do so. In practice it may take a little longer. But when I say "all" that is precisely what I mean.

"In the first year of my Presidency I shall close down, that is, disarm and evacuate, all our military bases abroad; and hand them over either to the host country, or, if the hosts agree, to the United Nations. All our warships will return to their home ports, tasked with patrolling our own shores, not those of other nations. I believe that our friends in Europe, Japan and Korea are eminently capable of looking after their own defense."

This was the moment the Republicans chose. The party leaders in the House and the Senate exchanged signals and then stepped forward, bowed to the chair, and marched out. One by one the Republicans followed until there were just six of them left. The Democrats sent them on their way with ironic applause and subtle abuse. The Chair called for order. The President waited patiently. When they had all left the chamber, she resumed her address without making any reference to the incident, except to ask, "Now where was I?" as she searched her papers.

"No one," she said, "No one, should see the withdrawal of our forces as a defeat or as any reflection whatsoever on the courage and devotion to duty of the men and women who have served and continue to serve in the Army, Navy, Air Force and Marine Corps of the United States of America. I honor them for their service to our country. And in honoring them, let me promise that appropriate measures will be taken to protect the immediate and long-term interests of all our returning and retiring servicemen and women. Like the citizens of Iraq and Afghanistan, many of them bear the scars of traumatic conflict in which they should never have been involved. We have not treated the veterans of earlier wars well. We need to do better this time, much better; much, much better."

She insisted that she was not adopting a policy of isolationism. America would remain an integral part of the wider world. Her firm intention, she said, was to use the best qualities of America to offer leadership to the people of that wider world. She repeated her promise that it would be a leadership based on different principles than those adopted in the past: it would be a moral leadership, dedicated to overcoming world problems, particularly those of the environment, of poverty and of world peace.

"We shall take the lead in a massive worldwide 'swords to ploughshares' program," she said, "including phased total nuclear disarmament and conversion of armaments industries, both at home and abroad, to peaceful purposes."

She characterized the Middle East, Israel and occupied Palestine, as a "festering wound that has infected the body politic of much of our world."

The so-called "two state solution," she said, was clearly no solution to anything and would no longer receive American support.

"In its stead," she said, "I propose to use all the means at my disposal to persuade the parties to negotiate, in a broadly representative national convention, the constitution of a single secular state within the pre-1948 boundaries of Palestine, a constitution that will guarantee full protection for both individual human rights and for the rights of all religious communities."

She promised to support "an urgent and just solution to the plight of the Palestinian refugees."

She said she could see no justification for continuing American sanctions against Cuba. These would be lifted as soon as the necessary paperwork could be completed. The existence of an American military base on Cuban soil was an anomaly and an insult to the people of that island, whose friendship she proposed to cultivate. Like the other U.S. bases abroad, that at Guantánamo Bay would be handed back to the host government.

"On the home front," she said, "we shall take immediate,

and necessarily painful, steps to reduce our contribution to climate change. We shall impose strict controls on the use of coal for the generation of power. We shall introduce a new tax on gasoline, designed to reduce automobile usage. We shall lend vigorous support to the rapid expansion of wind, solar and geothermal power, to the expansion of rail transport and to the more efficient use of road transport. Regarding the expansion of nuclear power, I am leaving my options open pending an urgent wide-ranging public debate on the pros and cons."

She said that the U.S. government would treat substance abuse as a health problem and would take the lead in undermining the criminal control of the drug trade by decriminalizing it. She thought that this might be one of the few fields in which a state monopoly might be justified. She promised to listen to those who make a living from growing coca and poppies, with a view to offering them attractive alternatives. At home, registered addicts would be permitted to purchase their requirements from authorized dealers and would be encouraged to seek professional help to free them from the grip of their addictions and those who exploit them. Small scale recreational use of drugs would be strongly discouraged but would no longer be illegal, as in the case of tobacco and alcohol.

"In spite of the economic problems of recent years," she said, "the United States remains the richest country in the world. And yet we continue to worship the fetish of growth. For most of us it is a meaningless economic statistic. The statisticians tell us that the macro economy is growing but ordinary Americans see no corresponding improvement in the quality of their lives. And the macro economy grows, almost inevitably, at a cost to our environment. I put it to you that as a nation we are plenty rich enough. What we need is not growth, but maintenance and repair. To achieve this there will have to be a redistribution of wealth through taxation."

"One of the less attractive features of our capitalist economy," she said, "is a pervasive but often unacknowledged sense of insecurity, a fear of poverty, particularly poverty resulting from ill-health or old age. The insurance industry is one that profits from that sense of insecurity. That is why big insurance fears competition from a well-run, well-funded single payer national health insurance scheme. My administration will mobilize and lead the majority of our citizens who want to see such a scheme installed and working. We shall use the Canadian and various European national health services as our model, identifying the best features in each and adapting them to our needs."

"The rich," she went on, "may fear ill-health and old age as much as the poor, but their wealth provides them with a protective cushion. And yet they are still driven to go on accumulating, accumulating, building up stores of assets far greater than they could manage to spend, even in their most profligate advanced years. What drives them? What else but greed, greed for more and more wealth and greed for the power that that wealth gives them. It is obscene that in a country with, according to one estimate, over 16 million millionaires, one million of our children often go to bed hungry. Is it right that we allow great wealth to co-exist with such poverty? My administration will take steps to reduce the gap between rich and poor in our country.

"Let me put my cards on the table: I believe that all private participation in the fields of health, basic education, the provision of water and electricity and the provision of prisons should either be in the public sector or, at the very least, subject to strong public management and control."

"I hereby declare war," she said. "I declare war on poverty and hunger, on disease and ill-health, on unemployment, on climate change, and on unnecessary incarceration. I ask you to endorse that declaration."

She looked at her wrist-watch.

"I think I've given you enough to chew on for one day. My other obligations call. I ask you now to proceed to deliberate upon and send to me for my signature the *Act to Restore Democracy to the United States of America* which I have laid before you."

EIGHT

As the President finished that remarkable address, the Acela approached Washington Union Station. My colleague Tom Edwards was waiting for me. We stowed my gear in the trunk of his car and walked to the Mall. I had been there for Barack Obama's Inauguration, but the scene that met my eyes was something quite different. At the request of the President-elect, the Regional Director of the National Park Service had issued a general waiver of the regulations covering activities on the Mall during the Inauguration. Though it was mid-winter the place had all the appearance of an enormous summer camp. Neat rows of tents stretched into the distance. Banners fluttered between trees, bearing political slogans or the names of small towns or organizations. Pictures of President Michelle decorated tree trunks. Circles of men and women sat around charcoal braziers. Children ran up and down playing games that their parents thought had become obsolescent in the era of TV and the Internet. Groups of activists, led by banners proclaiming their creed, passed by shouting slogans, soliciting funds and signing on members. On large screens we saw Paul Jay of the Real News Network interviewing notabilities of the Left: Danny Glover, Cornel West, Michael Moore, Cedric Robinson. What chance did President Michelle's *Act to Restore Democracy* have of passing through Congress, he wanted to know. And who was the most likely candidate to succeed Joe Biden? One screen had been rented by an organization of citizen journalists and here the faces of both the interviewers and the interviewees were unfamiliar.

"Choose the next Vice-President," proclaimed a banner outside a large tent. We joined the line of voters. The touch-screens inside offered us a long list, Dennis John Kucinich, Ralph Nader and Hillary Clinton amongst them, with a space for write-ins, where some prankster had added "Sarah Palin." I stationed myself at the exit and recorded short interviews with the departing voters, an informal exit poll.

Nader seemed to be a favorite but his age, 79 in February, was held against him.

There was an intriguing rumor about Nader circulating that I haven't yet been able to verify. In 2009 he published a 731-page novel called "Only the Super-Rich Can Save Us!" in which a cabal of billionaires, judged to be progressive, Warren Buffet, George Soros, Bill Gates and the like, set out to use their money and influence to reform the United States. That much is fact, at least the publication of the novel is fact, not the fictional content.

The rumor had it that President Michelle had charged Nader with assembling just such a secret cabal to prepare for the stock market crash which seemed likely once the new administration's policies were revealed. Their task would be to use their skills and fortunes to acquire controlling interests in strategic sectors of the economy. They would buy stocks at rock-bottom prices and subsequently make them over to transparently managed, publicly owned holding companies. The board members who would be appointed to represent the public interest would, at worst, have access to the corporations' confidential data. At best, they would be able to bend company policies towards conformity with those of the administration.

The right wing radio talk shows were alive with a host of similar conspiracy theories. Only time will reveal how much truth they contain.

Meetings were in progress everywhere, announced on Facebook and Twitter and mobile loud hailers. The digital social networks seemed to have taken on a human form, person to person. Digital acquaintances discovered the real faces that belonged to familiar network names. Everyone in the Mall seemed to belong to some activist committee or to be involved in some supporting task. Even the kids. The informal ban on alcohol and drugs appeared to be working and yet everyone seemed to be on a permanent high.

"This is real democracy at work," was Tom's reaction.

"But is it sustainable?" I wondered aloud.

Beyond that, I had no time for analysis. I was too busy collecting material for this book and my classes.

The activists' central concern seemed to be whether Congress would agree to pass the President's *Act to Restore Democracy*. Pressure groups were formed to target members of Congress and the Senate who were perceived to be waverers. In mobile truck-mounted printing shops and nearby Washington offices, they printed a poster about each legislator listing lobby influence, personal wealth and the source of campaign funds. Then they sent these same legislators invitations to meet with their constituents down on the Mall. The progressive legislators emerged from the Capitol. I attended some of the lively discussions which ensued.

One Senator issued a counter invitation, offering to receive a delegation in the centrally heated comfort of his office. Retiring to his Washington abode that evening, he found his domestic peace disturbed by rowdy picket lines. The publicity was embarrassing and the next day he put on his overcoat and took a walk.

The media, foreign, national and local, had a field day. For the first time in years, sales of newspapers increased. Previously unknown activists became celebrities overnight. Television screens beamed a stream of comment and discussions and interviews.

Inside the Capitol, the House and the Senate began their separate consideration of the *Democracy* bill. The activists were determined to maintain a substantial presence on the Mall until the Act had passed to the President for signature. Reluctant departures were balanced by new arrivals, eager to participate in what was seen as, to use a frequently heard cliché, "the making of history."

The corporations, the lobbies and the right wing think tanks had been taken by surprise but it only took them a day or two to mobilize their resources, pouring millions of dollars into media campaigns against the *Act*. The legislators, until now beneficiaries of their largesse, were caught between the proverbial rock and a hard place. Support for the bill offered them an uncertain future, which many must have been reluctant to face; but if the bill passed, in spite of their opposition, where would that leave them? The lobbyists nibbled at the edges of the Democratic vote. The outcome was by no means clear.

NINE

Tom and I sat beside a brazier on the Mall late that evening, chatting to friends. Our attention was suddenly directed to nearest screen by a call "Watch this, watch this." The announcer said that they were going to break their program to play a clip that had just appeared on YouTube.

What we saw then was a gang dressed in the white hoods and cloaks of the Klu Klux Klan, bearing flaming torches and manhandling and frog marching a black woman. As they lifted her onto a platform and tied a rope around her neck, it became clear that the object of their lynching was a life-like effigy of President Michelle. The table was removed and the effigy swung free. Those assembled raised a great cheer. As they began to sing the National Anthem, the clip was cut short.

TEN

The next day the President's new press secretary, Jim Bates, announced that President Michelle had issued an invitation to the unsuccessful Republican candidate, Sarah Palin, to form a small committee, selecting the members herself, to advise the President. President Michelle undertook to spend a private hour with this committee once a month. She would listen to its advice, said Bates, but of course (and he smiled a wan smile) did not promise to act on it.

That piece of political gamesmanship put the Republicans in a quandary. Fox News saw the offer as a poisoned chalice and warned Ms. Palin to reject it out of hand. More moderate Republicans were afraid that rejection would send the wrong message to swing voters. Ms. Palin vacillated.

Asked about the mock lynching, Bates deplored it in the strongest terms. YouTube had done the right thing, he said, by removing the offending clip as soon as it was drawn to their attention. He said he understood that most of the perpetrators had already been arrested. The President had authorized him to say that once the circumstances surrounding the incident became clear she would give serious consideration to bringing those responsible to Washington to explain, in public if that seemed appropriate, what their motives were. If the law had been broken, criminal proceedings would follow. However, her feeling was that the law alone was inadequate to deal with such lost souls. And there, for the time being, the matter has rested.

President Michelle's first two major speeches attracted front page headlines throughout the world. On its cover Time Magazine announced *The Second American Revolution*. The Jerusalem Post had *Michelle Obama Threatens Israel's Existence*. The Johannesburg Mail and Guardian welcomed *A President for all the World*.

The new Pope, the first black man to be elected to that office, congratulated the new President, the first black woman to be elected to that office, but made no public comment on her speeches, in which she had made mention of the abortion issue.

The British Prime Minister, David Cameron, conveyed to the President the hope that the special relationship between their two countries would be maintained.

There are few female presidents. All of them sent warm sisterly greetings. Perhaps the warmest came from the only African female head of state, President Ellen Johnson-Sirleaf of Liberia.

Hugo Chavez, Evo Morales and the aging Castro brothers were amongst those who also sent warm messages of welcome and support.

Throughout the world, Barack Obama's election had raised hopes amongst ordinary folk who had been deeply cynical about their own political leaders. Many of these had soon been disillusioned by what they perceived to be his failure to meet his campaign promises and by his selection of old guard politicians as his advisers.

Michelle Obama had made no campaign promises. Now what was seen as her courageous departure from the tarnished politics of the past served to spark their imagination again. In capital city after capital city and in smaller towns, hundreds of thousands turned out in response to the promise that her speeches seemed to offer. Apart from a few transparently opportunistic attempts to join the bandwagon, the traditional mainstream parties played little part in this. In Europe, the pro-Michelle rallies passed without incident. Those in Moscow and Cairo, Teheran and Beijing were dispersed with water cannon. In Addis Ababa and Abuja and Harare, political leaders who attempted to address the rallies had to be rescued by their armed escorts. All survived but with their Mercedes Benzes scratched and dented and, in one case, the windscreen smashed.

ELEVEN

On day 7 after the Inauguration, the world's attention shifted to the Middle East. Throughout the occupied Palestinian territories, unarmed people were assembling in groups and setting out to march on Jerusalem. The slogans on their tee-shirts read "Shoot me" and "I am not afraid to die" in Arabic, Hebrew and English. One banner read, "This is the third and last Intifada." (It was 25 years since the launching of the first Intifada.) Most of the marchers were young Palestinian men but they included women (some in slacks, some more modestly dressed, with head-scarves) and children, with a sprinkling of Israelis and foreign activists. Some carried images of President Michelle and of Yasser Arafat and banners with slogans like "One state, one person, one vote," and "Palestine, 1948." Maariv reported that IDF security cameras had identified the daughter and sons of Marwan Barghouti in the vanguard of four of the marches.

From their remotely controlled observation posts, the Israeli loudspeakers issued orders to disperse. The marchers sat down, filling the road behind the control barrier at every checkpoint. The loudspeakers issued dire warnings. The Palestinians would have only themselves to blame for their failure to do as they were told. The marchers ignored the warnings and waited patiently for the television cameras to arrive.

In Jerusalem Israel's cabinet sat in almost permanent session, issuing reassuring official statements which failed to conceal what must have been deep concern about the change in American policy.

The stalemate was broken when a young Palestinian marcher evaded the marshals and scaled a barrier. A nervous Israeli conscript, monitoring the action on a computer screen in a concrete bunker a mile away, used her mouse to focus the cross-hairs on her target and pressed a key, issuing an instruction to a remotely controlled gun to fire. The young man fell to the ground. The enraged demonstrators, defying their marshals, attacked the barrier.

In the bunker, a reserve officer gave the order to fire on the multitude, but one young conscript cried out, "No, no, don't shoot. Let them through."

The enraged officer ordered, "Arrest her!"

The mutinous conscript, gaining courage from her own spontaneous action and with nothing to lose now, urged her fellows to hold their fire, arguing that the Palestinians appeared to be unarmed and also that there might be some Israeli activists in their ranks. A heated discussion ensued, but in the event, no further shots were fired. The marchers poured through, heading for the next barrier.

One reservist was a journalist. He broke all the rules and phoned this story through to a radio station. Censorship breached, news of the mutiny spread rapidly to every Israeli bunker in the Occupied Territories, no doubt sparking further heated debate. Deprived of the protection of a friendly U.S. government, both the conscripts and their officers now had to weigh their action against the very real prospect of being charged with war crimes in an international court.

In Tel Aviv, a mass meeting in the square which had seen the assassination of Yitzchak Rabin, passed resolutions in support of the mutineers by acclamation and called on the government to let the marchers through.

On their hilltops, the Israeli settlers watched anxiously and polished their rifles, preparing for combat. But against whom? And who would fire the first shot?

42

TWELVE

Eight days after Michelle Obama's inauguration as President, the *Act to Restore Democracy to the United States of America* received the approval of the House of Representatives and the Senate and was sent to her for signature. She signed it without delay.

That same evening, she took her daughters, Malia and Sasha, for a walk on the Mall, accompanied by every member of her cabinet-in-waiting and three others, the Rev. Jeremiah Wright, Ralph Nader and Ohio Congressman Dennis Kucinich. The Head of the United States Secret Service must have had a fit, but for the participants, it was a jamboree. After an hour of shaking hands and hugging old friends, President Michelle mounted a small stage. Her image appeared on the large screens and nationwide.

"My fellow Americans," she said. "I am not going to say thank you. That would imply that you have done this for me. Rather, I suggest that we all congratulate ourselves on a job well done. And let us resolve that in a hundred days and again in a year's time and two years' time, and four years' time we will again be able to put our hands on our hearts and congratulate ourselves on another job well done. We have much to do. But already we have a story to tell. Sleep well tonight in your tents and sleeping bags. Dream pleasant dreams and tomorrow morning, go home to America and tell your stories, our stories. Go with all my love. And God bless you all."

Then she raised her right hand, palm facing the crowd and the cameras, as if to still the applause.

"From this day on," she said, slowly making a fist and looking up at it, "this has a new meaning. No longer 'black power,' but 'people power.'"

And the crowd responded, raising their fists and calling, "People power. People power."

THIRTEEN

On the ninth day after her Inauguration, President Michelle addressed the members of the Senate and the House of Representatives for the third time.

She congratulated them first for passing the *Act to Restore Democracy to the United States of America.*

"Now it falls to me," she said, "to introduce to you my nominee for the august post of Vice-President of the United States of America."

She paused and let her gaze wander over the assembled legislators, keeping them in suspense.

"I really have no need to introduce him," she said at last. "You already know him well. He is one of you. Congressman Dennis Kucinich, please step forward."

That evening Joe Biden gave an interview, explaining his resignation. He started by expressing his abiding respect and affection for both Presidents Obama. His problem was that the radical new policies which were being pursued had no mandate from the American people. They were the policies of a secret cabal, still largely unidentified, and not those of the Democratic Party. While he was not without sympathy for some of the measures President Michelle planned to introduce, he felt that the ends could never justify the means.

The interviewer reminded him that President Michelle had stated that she did not intend to stand for re-election in 2016 and asked him whether he would be a candidate in four years' time. He refused to commit himself.

FOURTEEN

I have a deadline to meet. As I bring this account of President Michelle Obama's first ten days in office to a close, news is coming in from Jerusalem. The marchers have at last reached their destination and are assembling on al-Haram al-Sharif (aka the Temple Mount), perhaps a million of them. Several unconfirmed reports say that Marwan Barghouti will come out of hiding to address them and that his wife Fadwa Ibrahim will also speak. Ahmad Sa'adat may join them. The television cameras show the crowds parting to give passage to small groups of Israelis displaying banners inscribed with slogans of solidarity.

Al-Jazeera reports that Barghouti will demand the immediate release of all political prisoners and the calling of a national convention to draw up a constitution for a secular Palestinian state within the 1948 pre-partition boundaries. According to Haaretz the Israeli cabinet is deeply divided and the IDF has returned to barracks, refusing to undertake further policing duties. The withdrawal of automatic American support has thrown the Israeli body politic into disarray. Existing parties are falling apart and new alliances are emerging, some prepared to work with the Palestinians, some intransigent. A sign of the times is that there are no uniformed Israelis to be seen on the Temple Mount. It is not clear what the settlers plan to do.

FIFTEEN

When I was a child, one of my favorites amongst my mother's bed-time stories concerned an itinerant mechanic who chanced upon the abandoned workshop of a deceased puppet master. The young mechanic lifted a pretty marionette from its hook on the wall and when her joints creaked, took out his oil-can and applied a drop of oil to each. At once the marionette began to dance and sing. To cut a long story short, the two of them succeeded in bringing life to all the stiff-jointed puppets in that workshop and then to their fellows all over the world.

Is there a chance that Michelle Obama, by lubricating creaking political joints in the United States will set in train a similar process?

Big business and its allies dispose of enormous resources and will not submit to defeat without a struggle. In forcing through the *Democracy Act*, President Michelle and her allies have won the first battle. Much will depend on what they manage to achieve in the two years before the 2014 mid-term election. If the changes of policy and new legislation fail to result in meaningful economic improvements and more jobs, fickle American voters might well sweep aside the Democratic Party's overwhelming majority in Congress. And then, what?

In the longer term the military withdrawal and disarmament

the President proposes, promise a major reduction of government expenditure. If American industry responds to her urgent challenge to convert the country's power base from dependence on fossil fuels to renewable energy with vigor and inventiveness, it might yet lead the world in a new industrial revolution. But that is a very big "if."

On the downside, there is always the chance that the international network of terrorists will see her election as a victory for them and an encouragement to launch new anti-Western adventures.

What does the future hold? Ten days after Michelle Obama's inauguration as the first woman to be elected President of the United States of America it is much too early to tell.

The only prediction one can make with any confidence is that we have interesting times ahead of us.

BY THE SAME AUTHOR

Ama: a Story of the Atlantic Slave Trade
by Manu Herbstein
**Winner of the 2002 Commonwealth Writers Prize for the Best
First Book**

"I am a human being; I am a woman; I am a black woman; I am an African. Once I was free; then I was captured and became a slave; but inside me, I have never been a slave, inside me here and here, I am still a free woman."

In the course of four hundred years some twelve million Africans were forcibly transported across the Atlantic to serve European settlers and their descendants. Only the barest fragments of their stories have survived. Manu Herbstein's ambitious, meticulously researched and moving novel sets out to recreate one of these lives, following Ama, its eponymous heroine, from her home in the Sahel, through Kumase at the height of Asante power, and Elmina, center of the Dutch slave trade, to a sugar plantation in Brazil.

"This is story telling on a grand scale," writes Tony Simões da Silva. "In *Ama*, Herbstein creates a work of literature that celebrates the resilience of human beings while denouncing the inscrutable nature of their cruelty. By focusing on the brutalization of Ama's body, and on the psychological scars of her experiences, Herbstein dramatizes the collective trauma of slavery through the story of a single African woman. *Ama* echoes the views of writers, historians and philosophers of the African diaspora who have argued that the phenomenon of slavery is inextricable from the deepest foundations of contemporary western civilization."

The Boy who Spat in Sargrenti's Eye
by Manu Herbstein
**Winner of the African Literature Association's 2016 award
for the Creative Book of the Year**

Sargrenti is the name by which Major General Sir Garnet Wolseley, KCMG (1833 – 1913) is still known in the West African state of Ghana.

Kofi Gyan, the 15-year old boy who spits in Sargrenti's eye, is the nephew of the chief of Elmina, a town on the Atlantic coast of Ghana. On December 25, 1871, Kofi's godfather gives him a diary as a Christmas present and charges him with the task of keeping a personal record of the momentous events through which they are living. This novel is a transcription of Kofi's diary.

Elmina town has a long-standing relationship with the Castelo de São Jorge da Mina, known today as Elmina Castle, built by the Portuguese in 1482 and captured from them by the Dutch in 1637. In April, 1872, the Dutch hand over the unprofitable castle to the British. The people of Elmina have not been consulted and resist the change. On June 13, 1873 British forces punish them by bombarding the town and destroying it. (It has never been rebuilt. The flat open ground where it once stood serves as a constant reminder of the savage power of Imperial Britain.)

After the destruction of Elmina, Kofi moves to his mother's family home in nearby Cape Coast, seat of the British colonial government, where Sargrenti is preparing to march inland and attack the independent Asante state. There Melton Prior, war artist of the London weekly news magazine, *The Illustrated London News*, offers Kofi a job as his assistant. This gives the lad an opportunity to observe at close quarters not only Prior but also the other war correspondents, Henry Morton Stanley and G. A. Henty.

Kofi witnesses and experiences the trauma of a brutal war, a run-up to the formal colonialism which would be realized ten years later at the 1885 Berlin conference, where European powers drew lines on the map of Africa, dividing the territory up amongst themselves. On February 6, 1874, Sargrenti's troops loot the palace of the Asante king, Kofi Karikari, and then blow up the stone building and set the city of Kumase on fire, razing it to the ground.

Kofi's story culminates in his angry response to the British auction of their loot in Cape Coast Castle. The loot includes the solid gold mask shown on the front cover of the novel. That mask continues to reside in the Wallace Collection in London.

The invasion of Asante met with the enthusiastic approval of the British public, which elevated Wolseley to the status of a national hero. All the war correspondents and several military officers hastened to cash in on public sentiment by publishing books telling the story of their victory. In all of these, without exception, the coastal Fante feature as feckless and cowardly and the Asante as ruthless savages.

The Boy who Spat in Sargrenti's Eye tells the story of these momentous events for the first time from an African point of view. It is told with irony and with occasional flashes of humor. The novel is illustrated with scans of seventy engravings first published in *The Illustrated London News*.

Prof. Trevor R. Getz of San Francisco State University, calls this novel "a compelling story of a young man caught in the midst of turmoil and change...a masterwork of historical fiction..."

Brave Music of a Distant Drum
by Manu Herbstein
A sequel to *Ama, a Story of the Atlantic Slave Trade*

This book is about a slave called Ama. She is old and dying but with an amazing tale to tell; she is blind and cannot write her story, so she tells it to her son. It is a tale of violence, heartache, a story of hope and courage, determination and ultimately love. It is a story of Ghana, of its wonderful people, stolen and taken to a foreign land. Ama—scream your story!!! Glenys Bichan, Cambridge High School Library, New Zealand

There are some stories that touch you and some that change you. This is what Kwame Zumbi discovers after a visit with his blind mother…Award-winning author Manu Herbstein blends fact with fiction to create a rich story that not only tells a heart-wrenching and powerful tale of friendship, love, and loss, but also chronicles the history of the trans-Atlantic Slave Trade and the scars that it has left behind. It's not an under-statement to say that Herbstein's tale is a vital part of history and a key to understanding cross-cultural relations today. Keilin Huang, papertigers.org

Manu Herbstein has written an incredible story about the life of Ama, born in Africa but now an aging and blind slave woman in Brazil. She is nearing the end of her life, but is determined she will not go to her grave until her story has not only been told, but written as well. This is a beautifully written, thought-provoking book about age-old questions involving man's inhumanity to man. Betty Kowall, Waterloo Region Record

What a beautiful follow up to "Ama." Talya Honor, Goodreads

Akosua and Osman
by Manu Herbstein
2011 BURT AWARD FOR GHANA

Akosua Annan is a confident and fiercely intelligent student at a posh Cape Coast school. There she comes under the influence of a charismatic feminist teacher.

Osman Said's background is very different. Upon the death of his parents, a police sergeant and an unschooled market trader, immigrants to Accra from the North, he is adopted by a retired school teacher, Hajia Zainab. After a spell as an apprentice in an auto workshop, he returns to school. There, finding the teaching inadequate, he becomes an avid reader and educates himself.

Akosua and Osman are thrown together by chance in the course of a school visit to the slave dungeon at Cape Coast Castle. Their paths cross again as finalists in the national school debating competition where the subject is "The problem of poverty in Ghana is insoluble." They meet for the third time as students at the University of Ghana and as we leave them, it looks as if their relationship might develop into something permanent.

"This fascinating novel tells the story of how these two young people from these disparate backgrounds are brought together as if by an unseen hand, in a process that teaches us about our history, our common humanity despite ethnic differences, the need to pursue our ambitions, the strength of human sexuality and the need for self-discipline, and, above all, the power of love." The Judges, Burt Award for African Literature, 2011.

Ramseyer's Ghost
by Manu Herbstein

Kwani? Manuscript Prize Longlist 2012

2050. The global village has disintegrated.

The Third World War, ending in a stalemate, has left the planet split between two hostile powers, each with a captive sphere of influence.

The Atlantic Ocean has become an American sea.

Responding to economic decline, the U.S. government has shed ballast, jettisoning areas and populations which make no contribution to the prosperity of its ruling class.

Manifest Destiny is once again the flavor of the day.

West Africa has become a desert of failed states and anarchy, dotted with mines and oil rigs, stockaded and armed by U. S. corporations.

Dumps of toxic waste litter the coast.

From their island outpost of São Tome, the Americans dispatch expeditions of geologists and mining engineers into the dangerous interior of the Dark Continent to search for untapped resources.

One such expedition has gone missing.

Ekem "Crash" Ferguson, born in the U.S. in 2008 of African parents and abandoned to the care of foster parents, is a Captain in the Marine Corps. His career blocked and his marriage failing, he accepts an offer to proceed to Ghana on a one-man mission to find the missing experts.

His arrival in Africa is inauspicious: in a shack amongst the coconut palms he comes across two human skeletons.

This is only the first of his many unexpected discoveries.